DreamWorks

# DRAGONS

# How to Track a DRAGON

adapted by Erica David

Ready-to-Read

Simon Spotlight
New York London Toronto Sydney New Delhi

SIMON SPOTLIGHT
An imprint of Simon & Schuster Children's Publishing Division
1230 Avenue of the Americas, New York, New York 10020
This Simon Spotlight edition May 2016

Manufactured in the United States of America 0416 LAK
2 4 6 8 10 9 7 5 3 1
ISBN 978-1-4814-6088-0 (hc)
ISBN 978-1-4814-6087-3 (pbk)
ISBN 978-1-4814-6089-7 (eBook)

There was trouble
at Dragon's Edge.
A Rumblehorn dragon
was up to no good.
Every night it attacked
the Dragon Riders' fort.

Hiccup and his friends set a trap.
They wanted to catch the dragon.
Instead, they caught Gobber!

Gobber had come from Berk
to talk to Hiccup.
He explained that Hiccup's father,
Stoick, was shouting at everyone.
"He's driving the village crazy!"

Hiccup had to go back to Berk.
He had to find out what was
wrong with Stoick.
He didn't want to leave with
a Rumblehorn on the loose,
but his dad was more important.

When Hiccup got to Berk,
he heard his dad shouting.
"I said I wanted these weapons
arranged by deadliness!" Stoick
yelled as he stomped away.

Hiccup followed his dad
across the village.
Stoick was being very
hard on everyone.

He even yelled at a nice old woman
named Gothi.
"You plow like an old woman!"
he shouted at her.

Hiccup soon realized what was wrong.
Stoick wouldn’t admit it,
but he missed his old dragon,
Thornado.
He spent a lot of time keeping
Thornado’s saddle nice and shiny.

Hiccup had an idea.
He asked his dad to help
with the Rumblehorn dragon.
Stoick loved a challenge!
It would make him feel better.

Meanwhile, back at Dragon's Edge,
Gobber hatched a plan.
He and the Dragon Riders
built a giant wall
to keep the Rumblehorn away.

But when the Rumblehorn
attacked again,
it slammed into the wall.
A tower fell on Gobber!
Gobber wasn't hurt, but he
began to act strange.
"Hello, loveys. Who'd like some
figgy pudding?" he asked.

“Hiccup, these Rumblehorn attacks are getting out of hand,” Astrid said when Hiccup and Stoick arrived.

Hiccup took charge.
He sent everyone out to search
for the Rumblehorn.

Hiccup and Stoick tracked the dragon through the forest.
“These footprints are fresh,” said Hiccup. “We should be right on top of the Rumblehorn.”
“It’s like the beast can sense us coming, and then it changes direction,” said Stoick.

Stoick had an idea for how
to draw the dragon out.
He sang loudly and beat the ground.
Soon the Rumblehorn appeared.
Stoick charged and lassoed the dragon
with his rope.

But the Rumblehorn didn't give up.
It took off into the air.
Stoick dangled from his rope!
The Rumblehorn flew higher
and higher.
Stoick tried to hold on,
but his hands slipped!
He fell through the air!

Hiccup and Toothless flew
to the rescue!
They caught Stoick, and then they
raced back to the fort.
What they didn't know was that now
the Rumblehorn was following them!

At the fort Gobber was still
acting strange.
He had even painted his face!
Suddenly the Rumblehorn swooped in.
It started following Gobber!
Gobber was still out of it.
He didn't see that he was in danger.

Hiccup and the others
tried to protect Gobber.
Astrid's dragon, Stormfly,
fired spikes at the Rumblehorn.
But the Rumblehorn wouldn't stop.

Everyone was worried.
They thought the Rumblehorn
would hurt Gobber.

But suddenly it stopped
and roared in Gobber's face.

“I think this dragon is trying to tell us something,” Stoick said. Slowly, he walked toward the Rumblehorn.

“What is it you really want, dragon?” asked Stoick.

The Rumblehorn roared again.
It tossed Stoick onto its back
and zoomed off into the sky.
The other dragons took flight.

From up high, Hiccup saw
the problem.
A giant wave was headed
for the island!
The Rumblehorn had been trying
to warn them!

Hiccup, Stoick, and the
Dragon Riders sped into action.
They built up Gobber's rock wall.
They made it longer and stronger
to block the wave.

The giant wave crashed
into the wall! The wall cracked!
The dragons and their riders worked
hard to plug the cracks.
The Rumblehorn helped too!
The fort was safe!

Later everyone was thankful
for the Rumblehorn.
“If he hadn’t been so hardheaded,
we would’ve been wiped out,”
Hiccup said.
Stoick smiled at the Rumblehorn.
“He is hardheaded, just like me,”
he said.

Stoick petted his new dragon.
“I think I’ll call you Skullcrusher,”
he told him.
Skullcrusher snorted happily.
He and Stoick made a great team.